20
RIG

# Amazing
# Lizards

# Amazing Lizards

WRITTEN BY
## TREVOR SMITH

PHOTOGRAPHED BY
## JERRY YOUNG

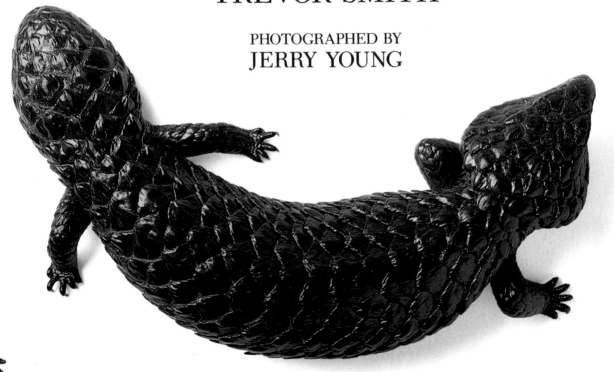

ALFRED A. KNOPF • NEW YORK

Conceived and produced by
Dorling Kindersley Limited

**Editor** Scott Steedman
**Art editor** Ann Cannings
**Managing editor** Sophie Mitchell
**Editorial director** Sue Unstead
**Art director** Colin Walton

**Special photography by** Jerry Young
**Illustrations by** Colin Woolf, Julie Anderson, and John Hutchinson
**Animals supplied by** Trevor Smith's Animal World
**Editorial consultants** The staff of the Natural History Museum, London

This is a Borzoi Book published by Alfred A. Knopf, Inc.

First American edition, 1990

Manufactured in Italy    0 9 8 7 6

**Library of Congress Cataloging in Publication Data**
Smith, Trevor
Amazing lizards / written by Trevor Smith;
photographs by Jerry Young.
p. cm. — (Eyewitness juniors; 7)
Summary: Features some of the remarkable members of the lizard
world, including the chameleon, flying gecko, and blue-tongued
skink, and describes the important characteristics of the whole group.
1. Lizards — Juvenile literature. [1. Lizards.] I. Young, Jerry, ill.
II. Title. III. Series.
QL666.L2S695   1990   597.95 — dc20   90-31884
ISBN  0-679-80819-1
ISBN  0-679-90819-6 (lib. bdg.)

Color reproduction by Colourscan, Singapore
Typeset by Windsorgraphics, Ringwood, Hampshire
Printed in Italy by A. Mondadori Editore, Verona

# Contents

# What is a lizard?

Lizards live in the warm parts of the world, from scorching deserts to steamy jungles. They are reptiles, like snakes, crocodiles, and dinosaurs. Lizards have hard, scaly skin, and most of them lay eggs.

**No hair, no sweat**
Lizards don't have hair or feathers to keep warm, and can't sweat to cool down. They are cold-blooded, which means their inside temperature is the same as the temperature of the air outside.

*Unlike snakes, most lizards have large ear openings*

**Look, Ma, no legs!**
Most lizards have four legs, but some have only two, and a few lizards have no legs at all. These legless lizards slither through the grass like snakes.

**Giant dragons...**
Water monitors like the one on this page can grow to be nearly 10 feet from head to tail. Komodo dragons from Indonesia get even bigger. One weighed 364 pounds – as much as you and three friends!

**...and a tiny gecko**
The smallest lizard of all is a gecko from an island in the Caribbean. It doesn't grow much more than 1.5 inches long, which makes it too small to wrap around a grown-up's thumb.

### May I have this dance?
When some male lizards fight, they stand up on their back legs and wrestle.

*A lizard's tough scales are made of the same substance as your toenails*

### Giant reptiles
The word *dinosaur* means "terrible lizard." But dinosaurs were very different from lizards. Dinosaurs had strong legs which held their bodies off the ground – unlike most lizards, which slither along with their legs sticking out at the side.

### Hungry?
There are 3,750 different kinds of lizard. Most eat insects, but the biggest ones prefer a lunch of pig or deer, and some are strict vegetarians.

*Some lizards' tails are four times as long as the rest of their bodies!*

### Leathery eggs
Some lizards give birth to live babies. But most lay eggs. Most lizard eggshells aren't hard like chicken eggs. Instead, they are soft and leathery and let in air as the little lizards grow inside.

9

# Chameleon

This bizarre lizard has feet like mittens, a tongue as long as its body, and eyes that swivel up and down. But most amazing of all is the way it changes color to escape enemies or sneak up on insects.

*Jackson's chameleon*

**Black with rage**
If you pester a chameleon, it may get so angry that it turns black.

**Born with horns**
Baby chameleons are only as long as your little finger. In one kind of chameleon, all males are born with small stumps on their heads. These stumps soon grow into horns.

**Hanging out**
The chameleon uses its long tail for balancing and climbing. It can even hang like a monkey, with its tail wrapped tightly around a branch.

## Island giant

There are 85 kinds of chameleon, and this is the largest one. It comes from an African island called Madagascar.

*Feet grip branches like a pair of pliers*

## Colorful feelings

The chameleon changes color for all sorts of reasons. It gets darker in the heat or sunlight, or redder to blend in with red bark. It also lets other chameleons know what mood it is in by changing color. If it loses a fight, a chameleon will hang its head and turn dark green.

## Lick that!

The chameleon keeps its tongue squashed up in a bundle in its mouth. Once it gets an insect in its sight, the lizard shoots its tongue out with lightning speed. The insect is trapped by the sticky pad on the end of the tongue. Then it is reeled in.

## Cross-eyed hunter

A chameleon's eyes don't always move together, so it can look at two things at once. As soon as one eye spots a fly, the other eye helps to focus on it.

11

# Blue tongues and tails

**M**any lizards use brilliant colors to scare or fool their enemies. The Australian blue-tongue lizard is dull gray on the outside. But when it opens its mouth, out pops a tongue of shocking blue.

## Throwaway tail

A lot of lizards can detach their tails when they're attacked. The tail wriggles in the grass and attracts attention – while the rest of the animal scoots away unnoticed!

*cracks*

*backbone*

## Cracked back

Lizards lose their tails with the help of special "cracked" bones in their backbones.

*scar from lost tail*

## Blue tail

A bright blue tail takes a bird's attention away from the more tender parts of this lizard's body. If it has to, the lizard can also detach its tail.

**Odd one out**
There are 10 lizards in the blue-tongue family. Strangely enough, one of them has a pink tongue!

**Menacing mouth**
The blue-tongue lizard tries to scare off enemies by opening its pink mouth, hissing, and waving its bright tongue around.

**Lick the air**
Like snakes, many lizards are always flicking their tongues in and out. They "taste" the air and pass all the flavors they find back to a special sense organ in the mouth.

**Sand swimmer**
Some of the blue-tongue's close relatives have nearly lost their legs. Instead of walking, they wriggle and "swim" through the sand.

**Lizard tongue sandwich**
In Sri Lanka, people used to believe that a lizard's wisdom was in its tongue. Children ate lizard tongue and banana sandwiches so they would grow up to be clever and well spoken.

# Leopard geckos

Geckos are great climbers and chatterers. There are over 800 kinds of gecko, and many of them make amazing sounds by clicking their tongues. Others, like these leopard geckos, never say a thing.

**Windshield wiper**
Geckos have long tongues. After a good meal of insects, a gecko will carefully clean its face – including its eyeballs – by licking itself!

**Well traveled**
Some geckos have spread halfway around the world, because they are not afraid of people and end up on ships heading for faraway spots.

**Forked tail**
When a lizard loses its tail, it grows a replacement right away. But the new tail is never the same as the old one, and some geckos will even grow a double or triple tail by mistake.

## Lucky bark
Geckos are common in houses in Asia. It is considered good luck if a gecko barks while a child is being born. So long as they hear the bark of the gecko, the family believes the house will be blessed.

## New outfit
Lizards change their skin regularly. Big flakes fall off to reveal the new layer that has grown underneath.

*Fringes on eyes keep out sand*

## Noisy
Some geckos make a lot of noise. They chirp, they bark, and they make the *geck-ooh, geck-ooh* sound that gives them their name.

*Tokay gecko*

## Wouldn't hurt a fly?
People in the Middle East used to fear leopard geckos because they thought the lizards had a poisonous bite. In fact, geckos are perfectly harmless (unless you are a beetle or a fly).

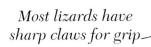

*Most lizards have sharp claws for grip*

# Two heads are better

What has two heads, eats snails, and looks like a pine cone? The shingleback lizard, that's what. Of course, it doesn't really have two heads – it just has a fat tail that it waves around to fool hungry birds into attacking the wrong end.

### Saving for a rainless day
When food is hard to find in the desert, the shingleback relies on the fat it has stored in its stubby tail.

### Garbageman
Shinglebacks live in the dry areas of Australia. They will eat just about anything they find there, from slugs and snails to ants, dead meat, fruit, and flowers.

### Beach umbrella
Why does it have such huge scales? No one knows for sure. But scientists think the scales may reflect heat to keep the shingleback cool.

**A deadly drool**
In the deserts of America lives
the Gila (HEE-luh) monster (above).
This fat, slow lizard is poisonous. It
hunts and defends itself by biting and
chewing a mixture of poison and spit
into its victim's flesh.

**Poor mom**
Instead of laying eggs,
the shingleback gives
birth to live babies.
The mother usually
has twins, and each
one is huge – about
half as long as she is.

*Shinglebacks vary in
color from greenish black to
brown with yellow spots*

*Spiny-tailed
lizard*

*Fat-tailed
gecko*
**Strange tails**
Many lizards, like the
fat-tailed gecko, store
food in their tails.
Others have
tails that are
covered in
sharp spikes,
and one
gecko has
a tail shaped
like a leaf.

*Leaf-tailed
gecko*

**You name it**
The shingleback
is also known as the
bobtail, stumpy-tail, pine
cone, or double-headed lizard.

# Flying gecko

Using its special flaps of skin like little parachutes, this tiny lizard can throw itself into the air and glide from tree to tree.

*skin patterns like lichen on a tree trunk*

**Flying dragons**
These Asian lizards have thin bones covered in skin that fold out from their sides. The dragons can't flap these "wings," but they can use them to glide for great distances.

**More flying dragons**
There are many stories of huge, evil, winged lizards that breathe fire and kidnap young maidens. Brave heroes like St. George set out to kill the dragon and rescue the maiden.

### Gecko feet

A gecko's toes are covered in thousands of microscopic bristles. These bristles hook into the smallest cracks, so the gecko can cling to walls and even walk across the ceiling.

### Blending in

When it is not gliding, the gecko lies flat against a tree trunk. To a passing bird it looks just like a piece of bark.

*flap along body*

*flattened tail for steering*

*webbed feet*

### Flying flaps

Stuck to a window, the gecko shows all the webs of skin that help it to glide.

### Eyes of a night hunter

The pupil is the black part of the eye that lets in light. At night, the gecko's pupils open wide so it can find insects in the dark. But in daylight, each pupil closes down to a row of tiny pinpricks.

### Treetops

Flying geckos live high in the trees in the jungles of Asia.

# Jesus Christ lizard

The basilisk lives by rivers and streams in the rain forests of Central America. The local people call it the Jesus Christ lizard, because it can walk (or rather run) across water.

*front legs (not used for standing) much weaker than back legs*

### Walking on water

The basilisk escapes from tight spots by getting up on its back legs and running. If it comes to a river or lake, it just keeps on going. The lizard's big feet and great speed stop it from sinking.

### Diving for cover

Basilisks don't just *walk* on water. They are also very good swimmers and can stay under water for half an hour to escape their enemies.

### Plumed basilisk

This lizard has a huge crest like a sail that runs along its head, body, and tail. Males have the biggest crests, which they raise to their full height whenever they get excited.

*The basilisk can use its long tail as an extra leg when it stands up*

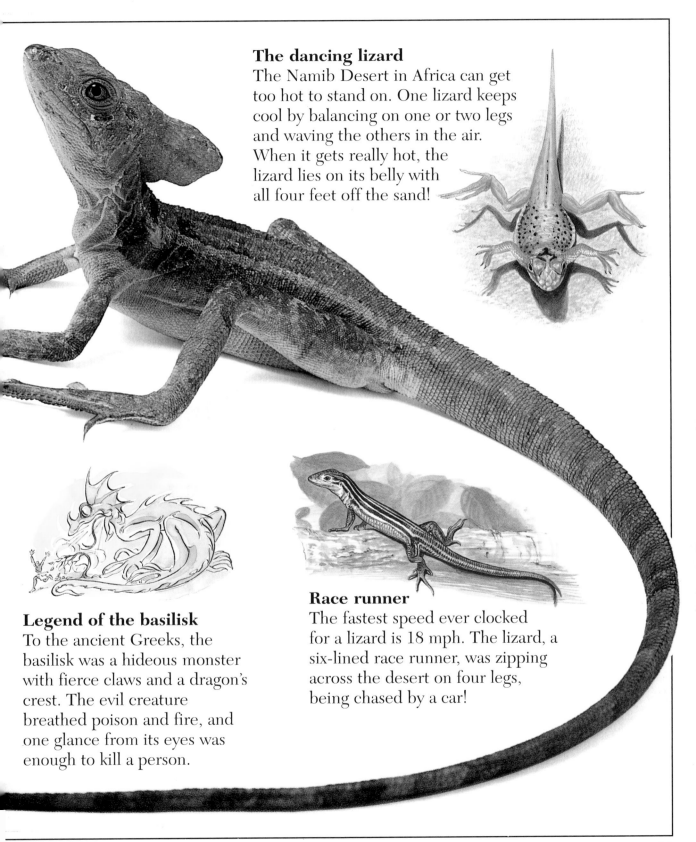

### The dancing lizard
The Namib Desert in Africa can get too hot to stand on. One lizard keeps cool by balancing on one or two legs and waving the others in the air. When it gets really hot, the lizard lies on its belly with all four feet off the sand!

### Legend of the basilisk
To the ancient Greeks, the basilisk was a hideous monster with fierce claws and a dragon's crest. The evil creature breathed poison and fire, and one glance from its eyes was enough to kill a person.

### Race runner
The fastest speed ever clocked for a lizard is 18 mph. The lizard, a six-lined race runner, was zipping across the desert on four legs, being chased by a car!

# A horned toad?

It is as ugly as a toad and is even known as the horned toad. But this little creature is really a lizard. It is covered in sharp spines that protect it from predators while it sits in the desert sun.

## Thorny devil

In the deserts of Australia lives a lizard that is just like the horned toad. It is called the thorny devil, and like the horned toad it eats ants by the thousands.

## Throat ticklers

The horned toad's main food is ants. It often sits near an ants' nest with its mouth wide open, gobbling up endless trails of the insects as they come out of the ground.

## High noon

Lizards are amazingly good at getting by in dry, desolate places. Horned toads are common in American deserts where it may not rain for months on end.

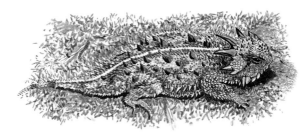

### Keeping out of sight
The horned toad is perfectly patterned to blend in with the desert rocks and sands. It also squats low to the ground, so that desert birds or foxes will not spot its shadow.

*In the evening, the lizard's skin color changes from light to dark brown to soak up more sunlight*

### Deadly collar
A snake or a bird would have a hard time swallowing a horned toad. Every inch of the lizard's skin is studded with spines, and it wears a collar of jagged spikes.

### Tears of blood
When it is attacked, the horned toad has the bizarre habit of squirting blood from its eyes. The jets of blood may sting attackers in the eyes or may just surprise them so much that they run away!

### Keeping moist
Every morning, the horned toad wanders around in search of dew, which it laps up with its long tongue.

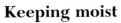

# Iguana

In South and Central America, iguanas are the biggest and most common lizards. They are found from deserts to rain forests, and there are more than 120 different kinds in the West Indies alone.

**Nasty tail**
This Mexican iguana has a long, spiked tail that it lashes at its enemies.

**Diving for seaweed**
The marine iguana is the only lizard in the world that feeds under the sea. After a good meal of seaweed, it suns itself on the rocks of the Galapagos Islands, off the coast of South America.

**Out of the egg**
The mother iguana lays her eggs under a log or in a hole in the ground. Then she leaves them. When the baby iguanas hatch, they have to look after themselves.

**Gums of steel**
The Galapagos Islands are also the home of huge land iguanas. These strange, lumbering lizards spend their days nibbling nothing but cactus.

**Any chips with that?**
Central American Indians have always been fond of iguana meat. You can even buy iguana burgers in snack bars in Panama.

24

## Rhinoceros iguanas

These enormous lizards have little horns on their foreheads. They may look fierce, but most of them eat nothing but plants.

## Courting colors

Many male iguanas are more colorful than the females. They use their flashy outfits to woo the females – who usually look quite bored by the whole performance!

*The flaps of skin that hang off an iguana's throat are called its dewlap*

# Tree dragon

The pricklenape agama lives high in the trees in mountain forests from China to Indonesia. With its long tail and powerful legs, this agile lizard can leap quickly and gracefully through the branches.

### This is *not* a lizard
It looks like a lizard, but the tuatara is more like a living fossil. It is the only survivor of a group of reptiles that were common at the time of the dinosaurs. Now it is found only on a few islands near New Zealand.

### Copying the chameleon
The pricklenape can change color from brown to green, to blend in better with the forest leaves.

*long tail used for balance in the treetops*

### Fringed toes
Like other lizards that live in trees, pricklenapes have very long toes with sharp toenails for clinging to branches. Their toes even have fringes of spiky scales for better grip.

The word pricklenape means spiky neck

Large eyebrows keep twigs and leaves out of eyes

## Lounge lizards
Lizards spend most of their time lounging around. So do some people, whom we call lounge lizards.

## Devil lizard
The toad-headed agama from Central Asia is so hideous-looking that when the local people painted the Devil, they used this lizard as a model!

## Chinese dragon
In China, the dragon is a wise animal that lives in the clouds and rivers. Chinese emperors used dragons as their symbols. When an emperor died, it was said he had ridden to heaven on the back of a dragon.

# Strange decorations

 Horns, spikes, crests, frills – lizards have found some bizarre uses for their hard layer of scales. Some use their ornaments for courting mates and scaring off rivals. Others have evolved some strange structures to protect themselves from hungry enemies.

## Bearded dragon

A lizard's tough covering of scales protects it like a suit of armor. The scales on this lizard's throat are long and pointed, and hang down in a strange "beard."

## Fold-out collar

The frilled lizard is an expert bluffer. It usually drapes its frill over its shoulders like a cape. But when it is cornered, the lizard hisses and extends its frill like a huge collar.

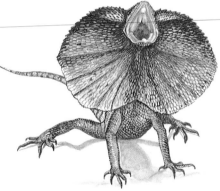

*scales*

*dead layer*

*living layer*

## Skin-deep

A lizard's scales are the top layer of its skin. They are like human hair or nails – dead on the outside, but growing down beneath the surface.

## Flashers in the jungle

Some male iguanas have brightly colored flaps of skin on their throats. They unroll the flaps, shocking rivals (or attracting females) with a flash of violent blue or orange.

**Look how big I am!**
When it feels threatened, the bearded dragon thrusts out its scaly "beard" and hisses and puffs like crazy.

*The lizard's "beard" usually hangs in folds from its throat*

*Boyd's water dragon*

**Horns and helmets**
Many male lizards have amazing horns and crests that females don't. They use them when trying to attract a mate or when fighting with other males.

*Lyre-headed lizard*

*Helmeted lizard*

*Mountain chameleon*

## Index